FINDING A COVID-19 VACCINE

by Fran Hodgkins

BrightP◆int Press

San Diego, CA

© 2021 BrightPoint Press
an imprint of ReferencePoint Press, Inc.
Printed in the United States

For more information, contact:
BrightPoint Press
PO Box 27779
San Diego, CA 92198
www.BrightPointPress.com

LIBRARY OF CONGRESS CATALOGING-IN-PUBLICATION DATA

Names: Hodgkins, Fran, 1964- author.
Title: Finding a COVID-19 vaccine / Fran Hodgkins.
Description: San Diego : BrightPoint Press, 2021. | Series: The COVID-19 pandemic |
    Includes bibliographical references and index. | Audience: Grades 7-9
Identifiers: LCCN 2020050065 (print) | LCCN 2020050066 (eBook) | ISBN 9781678200589
    (hardcover) | ISBN 9781678200596 (eBook)
Subjects: LCSH: Vaccines--Juvenile literature. | Vaccines--Research--Juvenile literature. |
    Vaccination--Juvenile literature. | COVID-19 (Disease)--Juvenile literature.
Classification: LCC RA638 .H63 2021 (print) | LCC RA638 (eBook) | DDC 615.3/72--dc23
LC record available at https://lccn.loc.gov/2020050065
LC eBook record available at https://lccn.loc.gov/2020050066

CONTENTS

AT A GLANCE

- Diseases are caused by bacteria and viruses. The virus SARS-CoV-2 causes COVID-19.

- The immune system protects the body from disease. It produces antibodies that recognize specific viruses.

- Some vaccines prepare the body to fight against viruses. There are three main types of viral vaccines. One uses live viruses. Another uses killed viruses. A third type uses the virus's RNA or DNA.

- Edward Jenner began creating a vaccine for smallpox in 1796. Today, many vaccines are given to children to protect them from diseases.

- Vaccines must be tested before they are approved by the Food and Drug Administration for use. They are first tested on animals. Then there are three phases of testing on human volunteers. Scientists make sure the vaccine is safe and effective.

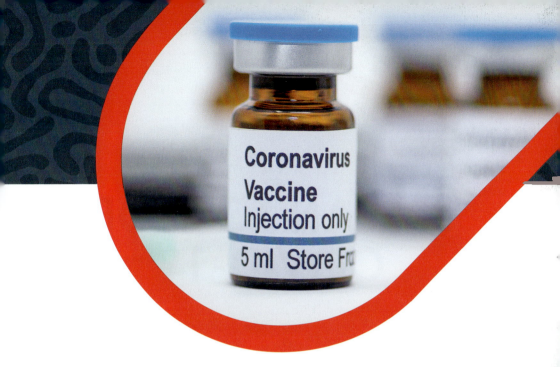

- The US government created Operation Warp Speed. This program made COVID-19 vaccine research, production, and distribution faster.

- The United States funded the medical companies Pfizer and Moderna. Both of these companies had promising vaccine trial results in November 2020.

- Russia and China both approved vaccines for limited use. Neither vaccine had completed phase three testing at the time of approval.

- The vaccine became a political issue for the 2020 presidential election. Experts worried that people wouldn't trust a vaccine when it was available.

A PLAN TO STOP COVID-19

On May 15, 2020, President Donald Trump held a conference at the White House Rose Garden. A team of medical experts stood behind him. Many of them wore masks. Audience members sat in chairs 6 feet (1.8 m) apart from one another. Masks and social distancing helped keep people safe from COVID-19.

President Donald Trump speaks about the coronavirus on May 15, 2020.

Social distancing is sometimes called physical distancing. More than 1 million people in the United States had tested positive for COVID-19 by this date.

Trump was about to speak about his plan to deliver a COVID-19 vaccine. The plan was called Operation Warp Speed. The US government would work to develop a vaccine against the deadly disease as quickly as possible. Operation Warp Speed described how the United States would handle vaccine research. It also had plans for how to quickly make and deliver a vaccine to Americans. This process usually takes several years. Trump hoped a vaccine would be ready by the end of 2020.

Operation Warp Speed brought together many government agencies. The US military

The Department of Defense was part of Operation Warp Speed. Early in the COVID-19 outbreak, the Department of Defense also helped give out food.

was also involved. Top medical experts and scientists were already hard at work on a vaccine. Trump praised their work. Creating a vaccine against COVID-19 was one of the largest scientific efforts in the United States.

Research was necessary to make sure a vaccine was safe and effective.

A vaccine would protect people from getting COVID-19. It would slow the spread of the disease. Early in the **pandemic**, many US states went into lockdown. Businesses such as shopping centers and restaurants closed. Health experts recommended people stay home as much as possible. By early May, many states began reopening. But businesses still had to follow new guidelines to keep people safe. People hoped a vaccine would let life return to normal.

Many businesses were forced to close because of COVID-19.

In the meantime, Trump encouraged people to fight through the hard times. People needed to be patient. They needed to continue wearing masks and social distancing. These practices would help slow the spread of COVID-19 before a vaccine was made.

CHAPTER ONE

WHAT IS A VACCINE?

Bacteria and viruses cause diseases. Both are too small to be seen by the naked eye. Bacteria are tiny living things. They enter a person's body. Then they cause disease by making chemicals called toxins.

Viruses are even smaller than bacteria. They invade living cells. They use the cells

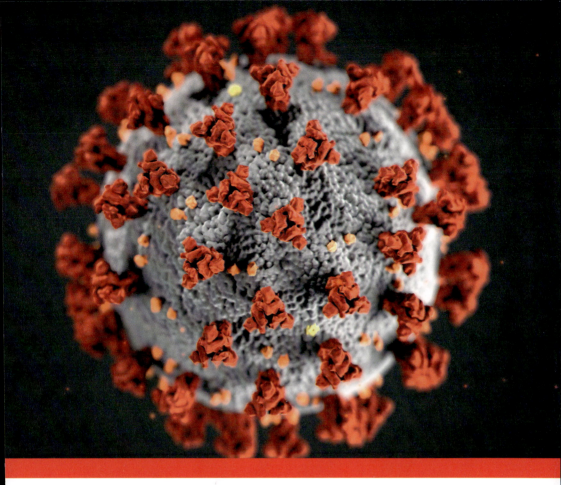

Viruses such as SARS-CoV-2 can cause disease.

to make copies of themselves. The cells die,

and the new viruses invade other living cells.

This process makes people sick.

Viruses contain genetic material such

as RNA or DNA. Genetic material has the

instructions that let viruses make copies of themselves. A protective coat surrounds the RNA or DNA.

COVID-19 is caused by the virus SARS-CoV-2. The body's immune system has special cells that attack and kill viruses such as SARS-CoV-2. They are called white blood cells, or lymphocytes. Two kinds of lymphocytes patrol the body: B cells and T cells. B cells watch out for invaders. When they find a virus, B cells make special molecules called **antibodies**. The shape of the antibody matches structures on the virus. The antibodies lock onto the virus

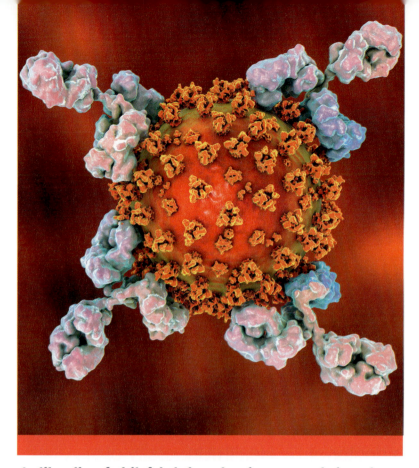

Antibodies (white) latch onto viruses and signal that they should be destroyed.

and signal for help. Then T cells come and destroy the virus.

The immune system makes different antibodies for each type of virus. It does not have the antibodies to fight a new virus at first. It takes longer to react. Scientists first detected SARS-CoV-2 in December 2019. People did not have antibodies to protect them from the virus. This allowed SARS-CoV-2 to spread quickly in people's bodies. "It gets in and hijacks the human cell's machinery," said Dr. Daniel Pastula, a doctor at UCHealth University of Colorado Hospital. "Instead of the cell doing what it's supposed to do, the virus . . . turns the [cell] into a machine to make more of the virus. It goes . . . until the immune system stops it," Pastula said.[1]

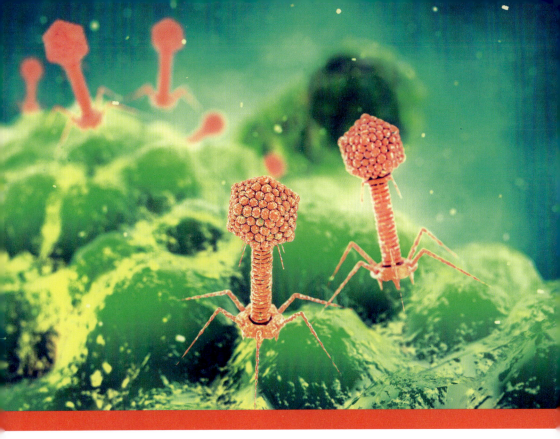

Each type of virus (red) has a different shape.

Vaccines help the body prepare to fight new viruses. They give the immune system a preview of the virus. The B cells produce antibodies. These antibodies are ready in case the virus returns.

TYPES OF VACCINES

There are three types of viral vaccines. The first type is the live attenuated vaccine. This vaccine contains live viruses. But the viruses are weakened and cannot cause disease. The immune system learns to build antibodies against them.

Other vaccines use killed viruses. The viruses cannot do any harm. The immune system learns from them. But its response is not as strong as with live attenuated vaccines. It may take additional doses to create immunity. These are called boosters.

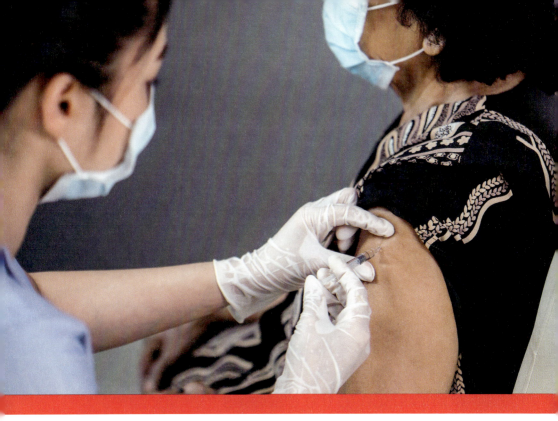

Medical professionals give patients vaccines so they are protected from certain diseases.

A third kind of vaccine uses part of the virus's RNA or DNA. As with the other types, it helps the immune system recognize a specific virus. The body produces antibodies. If a person comes in contact with the virus, the immune system is prepared to fight back.

Vaccines do not make people sick. They may cause minor side effects. These might include headaches, low fevers, and feeling tired. Such side effects are mild in comparison to the diseases that vaccines protect against. In rare cases, people may have severe allergic reactions.

Each vaccine protects people for different lengths of time. People who have received the measles vaccine are often protected for life. The polio vaccine is effective for eighteen years. The flu vaccine works for

approximately six months.

HISTORY OF VACCINES

In 1796, British scientist Edward Jenner

noticed that some milkmaids did not get

VACCINES DO NOT CAUSE AUTISM

In 1998, a British doctor wrote that the measles vaccine caused autism in children. Autism causes difficulties with communication and social behavior. Research by other scientists proved the doctor wrong. There is no link between vaccines and autism. But the damage had already been done. Some parents decided not to vaccinate their children. Their children could catch a preventable disease and spread it to others.

smallpox. Smallpox causes rashes that fill with pus. It can be deadly. All of the milkmaids had previously had a disease called cowpox. Jenner discovered that fluid from cowpox sores could protect people from smallpox. He used this information to create the first vaccine. Scientists today know that the cowpox virus and smallpox virus come from the same family of viruses. That is why exposing a person to cowpox gives immunity against smallpox.

Vaccine research advanced after the development of Jenner's smallpox vaccine. By the 1940s, certain vaccines were widely

Edward Jenner created the first vaccine.

distributed in the United States. Americans today receive six different vaccines before the age of four months. This protects them from deadly diseases such as measles and pertussis. These diseases once killed millions of people. Pertussis vaccines were created in the 1940s. A measles vaccine

followed in 1963. Deaths from these

diseases dropped sharply.

The World Health Organization (WHO)

monitors health around the world. The

organization helps countries treat disease

THE STORY OF POLIO

Polio is a viral disease that attacks the brain and spinal cord. It affects mostly children. At its peak in 1952, nearly 60,000 US children were infected. For most, there were only mild symptoms. But for about 1 percent of patients, polio caused paralysis. Paralysis is the inability to move. In 1955, Dr. Jonas Salk developed a polio vaccine. It contained killed viruses. The vaccine made a huge difference. The United States reported its last case of polio in 1979.

outbreaks. On May 8, 1980, WHO made an important announcement. Vaccination had officially wiped out smallpox. It had been about 180 years since Jenner's discovery. Now, the disease would no longer harm people. Vaccines made this achievement possible.

HOW VACCINES ARE TESTED

The federal government has rules to make sure vaccines are safe to use. Companies must carefully test vaccines before giving them to the public. Testing for all vaccines follows the same basic steps.

Vaccines are first tested on animals such as mice. Researchers will see if the vaccine creates an immune response. They figure out a safe starting dose. Scientists adjust the vaccine to make it more effective.

If the vaccine is successful, it advances to phase one of clinical trials. It is tested on twenty to one hundred people. They volunteer to be part of these trials. People volunteer because they know the vaccine will protect others. Volunteers are also paid for their participation.

Doctors make sure the volunteers are healthy. Illnesses could affect the trials.

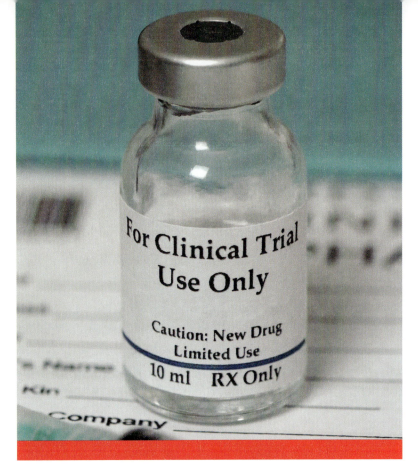

Vaccines go through several rounds of clinical trials before they can be approved for public use.

They could give researchers an incorrect picture of what is happening. Scientists note how healthy bodies respond to the vaccine. The vaccine is first given in low doses. Doctors make sure there are no side

Moderna was one of many companies around the world that worked to develop a COVID-19 vaccine.

effects. They may see if the vaccine is more effective at higher doses.

A vaccine moves into phase two if it is found to be safe in phase one. The vaccine is given to a larger group of people. Doctors may test it on people of different ages.

They want to make sure it is safe for as many people as possible.

If phase two is successful, the vaccine moves on to phase three. The vaccine is given to thousands of people. Some people are given a placebo instead. A placebo does not have any effect on illness. It does not protect volunteers from disease. Scientists compare these two groups. They see which group had more sick people. They hope there are many fewer sick people in the vaccinated group. This means the vaccine works.

Vaccines that pass phase three are approved by the Food and Drug Administration (FDA). The FDA is a part of the US government that oversees public health. Doctors watch their patients who got the vaccine. If it causes new side effects, the doctor will report these issues to the FDA. If problems are widespread, the vaccine may be **recalled**.

The testing and approval process takes time. For most vaccines, it takes about seven years. But COVID-19 infected millions of people within months. A vaccine for COVID-19 would save lives. But it still had

The FDA is the US government agency that approves vaccines and medicines for public use.

to go through testing trials. "We need to make sure any vaccines are both safe and effective," Dr. Pastula said. "To do all those checks will take at least a year."[2] Scientists raced to produce a vaccine in 2020. They knew people's lives would depend on their work.

CHAPTER TWO

HOW DID COVID-19 VACCINE RESEARCH BEGIN?

In December 2019, many people in Wuhan, China, became sick with pneumonia. Pneumonia happens when the lungs become infected and fill with fluid. It can make breathing difficult.

The first cases of COVID-19 were discovered in Wuhan, China.

At the time, the cause of the disease was unknown. But many of the first cases were linked to a seafood market in Wuhan. On December 31, Chinese officials contacted

WHO about the disease. The disease was later named COVID-19.

In late January 2020, Chinese officials placed Wuhan under lockdown. Nobody was allowed into or out of the city. But it was too late. COVID-19 was spreading around the world. On March 11, WHO declared COVID-19 a pandemic.

CORONAVIRUSES

Coronaviruses are a family of viruses. They have spikes on their surfaces that give them crown-like appearances. *Corona* means "crown" in Latin. Many of these viruses

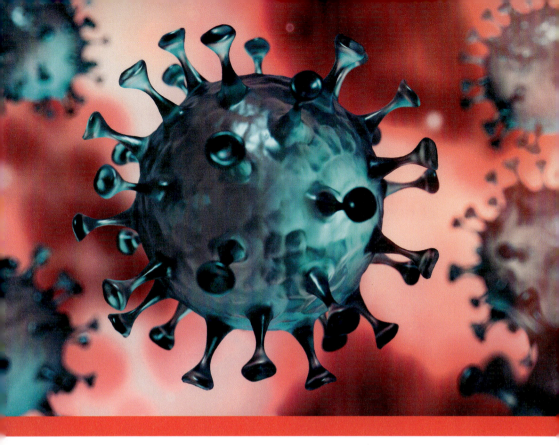

Some coronaviruses are known to cause diseases in humans.

cause **respiratory** symptoms such as

coughing or difficulty breathing.

Some coronaviruses have caused

disease outbreaks. Severe acute respiratory

syndrome (SARS) and Middle East

respiratory syndrome (MERS) are both

caused by coronaviruses. These diseases

sickened thousands of people. They also

had high death rates. Approximately

10 percent of SARS patients died. More

than 30 percent of MERS victims died from

the disease.

THE SARS-COV-2 GENOME

The first step to understanding SARS-CoV-2 was to record its genome. The genome is the complete list of the virus's genetic material. Scientists in China uploaded the SARS-CoV-2 genome online on January 12, 2020. It allowed scientists around the world to study the new virus. They learned that the virus started in bats. They could also see how the virus changed as it spread around the world.

COVID-19 is also caused by a coronavirus. *COVID* stands for "coronavirus disease." The number *19* is for the year the disease began, 2019. The virus that causes COVID-19 is named SARS-CoV-2. This stands for "severe acute respiratory syndrome coronavirus 2." It is closely related to the virus SARS-CoV, which causes SARS.

COVID-19 is milder than SARS and MERS. Scientists estimate that 0.6 percent of US patients die from the disease. But COVID-19 is much more **contagious**. Approximately 10,000 people became sick with SARS or MERS. But there were more than 50 million cases of COVID-19 in less than a year.

Knowledge about SARS and MERS helped scientists learn about COVID-19. They studied how the disease spread and

MERS AND SARS VACCINES

Scientists did research to make vaccines against MERS and SARS. But the research was never completed. No vaccines were made. Neither disease was as widespread as COVID-19. Most MERS cases were in the Middle East. SARS stopped spreading without a vaccine. The last known SARS case was in 2004. The research on other coronavirus vaccines gave scientists a starting point for a COVID-19 vaccine.

how to treat it. They used research on other coronaviruses to quickly begin developing a COVID-19 vaccine.

SYMPTOMS AND SPREAD

Like SARS and MERS, COVID-19 affects the respiratory system. Common symptoms of COVID-19 are coughing and a loss of smell. The disease is mild for most. But it can be very dangerous, especially for older people.

Even after someone recovers from COVID-19, the disease may have lasting effects. A person may experience a lingering cough, tiredness, and joint pain.

Patients with severe cases of COVID-19 may need to receive air from a machine.

Doctors and scientists continue to study

long-term effects of the disease.

Researchers also studied how the

virus spreads. SARS-CoV-2 is spread in

droplets. When people cough, sneeze, or

talk, droplets containing the virus leave their mouths and noses. Wearing a mask stops droplets from traveling through the air. The droplets can't land on people or surfaces. Standing 6 feet (1.8 m) apart from others also protects from droplets.

SARS-CoV-2 can stick to surfaces like door handles and railings. The virus may get on someone's hands. It enters the body when the person touches his or her eyes, nose, or mouth.

Handwashing is an easy way to protect against the virus. Soap breaks apart the protective coat around the virus.

Soap is able to destroy SARS-CoV-2 on hands and surfaces.

This destroys it. Dr. David Goldberg is

an assistant professor of medicine at

Columbia University. He says, "Soap

molecules disrupt the fatty layer or coat

surrounding the virus. Once the viral coat is

broken down, the virus is no longer able to function."[3]

OPERATION WARP SPEED

Many cities and states in the United States went into lockdown because of COVID-19. The Centers for Disease Control and Prevention (CDC) encouraged people to stay home. The CDC is a part of the US government that protects public health. COVID-19 affected everyday life. A vaccine was needed for life to return to normal.

The CDC and other parts of the US government created Operation Warp Speed. The goal was to produce and deliver 300 million doses of COVID-19 vaccines. They hoped to do this by January 2021.

Operation Warp Speed had three steps. The first step was to provide money to companies that were doing vaccine research. The US government selected fourteen companies. It gave each company millions of dollars. It later narrowed support to seven companies.

The US government also made plans to mass produce the vaccine. It can take a lot of equipment to do this. Companies needed

Millions of glass vials and syringes would be needed to deliver vaccines throughout the United States.

to make many doses in a short amount

of time.

Lastly, the operation described plans

to distribute the vaccine. Vials would be

needed to store doses. Doctors needed syringes to **inject** the vaccine. Companies began making these supplies before a vaccine was approved. It was important that every US state have access to the vaccine.

Vaccine development can take a long time. The Department of Defense (DOD) is a government agency that runs the military. It estimated that the normal vaccine process takes seventy-four months. Operation Warp Speed planned to develop, produce, and distribute the vaccine in just fourteen months. Government officials discussed vaccine progress on May 15, 2020. Mark

VACCINE DEVELOPMENT

The process of making a vaccine available to the public takes an average of seventy-four months. Operation Warp Speed hoped to have a vaccine ready in around fourteen months.

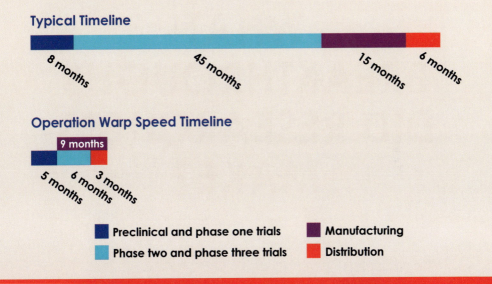

Typical Timeline

8 months

45 months

15 months

6 months

Operation Warp Speed Timeline

9 months

5 months

6 months

3 months

■ Preclinical and phase one trials
■ Phase two and phase three trials
■ Manufacturing
■ Distribution

"Operation Warp Speed Accelerated Vaccine Process," **Department of Defense**, *August 13, 2020.* **www.defense.gov.**

Esper was the secretary of the DOD at the time. He said, "Winning matters, and we will deliver . . . a vaccine at scale to treat the American people and our partners abroad."[4]

CHAPTER THREE

WHAT BREAKTHROUGHS DID RESEARCHERS MAKE?

Countries around the world rushed to develop a vaccine. Scientists researched many vaccines. Some used inactive forms of SARS-CoV-2. Others only used part of the virus's RNA. The first COVID-19 vaccines were tested on people

Scientists around the world worked to develop a vaccine for COVID-19.

in March 2020. Several were approved for

limited use in certain countries later that

year. But no vaccine had been approved for

full use by November 2020.

UNITED STATES

The US government provided nearly $10 billion toward a vaccine. This funding was part of Operation Warp Speed. Money went to companies such as Pfizer and Moderna. Both companies had vaccines in phase three trials by September 2020.

The Pfizer vaccine uses RNA from SARS-CoV-2. It is given in two doses. Pfizer promised at least 100 million doses of its vaccine to the United States. Phase three trials included more than 43,000 volunteers. On November 9, Pfizer shared its early phase three trial results. Its vaccine was more than 90 percent effective. Very few

people who got the vaccine later became

sick with COVID-19. Most volunteers who

got COVID-19 had received the placebo.

Pfizer later provided more specific numbers,

saying its vaccine was 95 percent effective.

TREATING COVID-19

A vaccine would protect people from getting COVID-19. But doctors needed to know how to treat people who had already become sick. New treatments also need to be tested before they can be used. On October 22, the FDA approved remdesivir for emergency use. The drug could only be given to COVID-19 patients who were in the hospital. Patients needed to be at least twelve years old to get remdesivir.

Pfizer was the first company to produce a vaccine with such positive results. The FDA approved the vaccine for emergency use on December 11. Distribution began on December 14. Pfizer hoped to vaccinate 25 million people by the end of 2020. But the Pfizer vaccine needed to be kept at −94°F (−70°C) in order to work. It would be difficult to deliver and store vaccines at this temperature.

The Moderna vaccine also uses SARS-CoV-2 RNA. And it is given in two doses. Its phase three trials had 30,000 volunteers. On November 16,

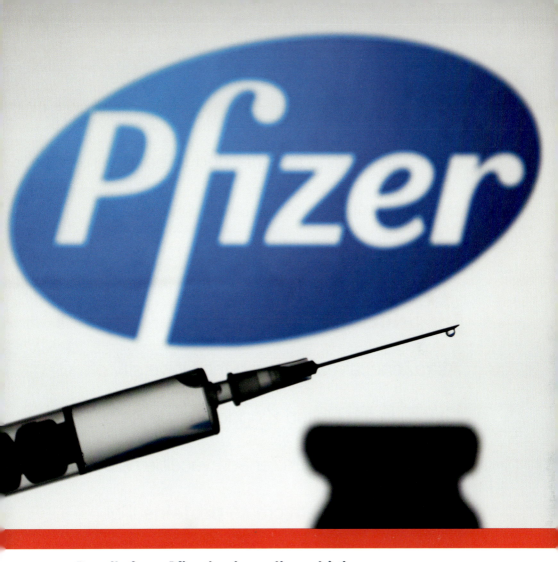

Results from Pfizer's phase three trials were promising.

Moderna announced that its vaccine was

94.5 percent effective. The company

applied for FDA approval of its vaccine

for emergency use on November 30. The Moderna vaccine also needed to be frozen. But the temperature required is similar to that of a normal freezer at −4°F (−20°C).

THE UNITED KINGDOM

AstraZeneca teamed with the University of Oxford in the United Kingdom to develop a vaccine. The AstraZeneca vaccine helps the immune system create **proteins** that defend the body against the virus. The UK government had ordered 100 million doses of the vaccine. This vaccine would be easier to distribute than the Pfizer and Moderna vaccines. It did not need to be frozen.

A screen in London, England, displays a message from Queen Elizabeth thanking health care workers for their work during the pandemic.

The AstraZeneca vaccine is given in two doses. During phase three trials, most volunteers were given two standard doses. But some received the first dose at half strength by mistake.

On November 23, the company released its phase three results. The vaccine was 62 percent effective at two standard doses. It could be around 90 percent effective when the first dose was given at half-strength. Researchers continued to study the people who received a half-strength dose. They needed to know if actually gave more protection against COVID-19.

The United Kingdom approved the Pfizer vaccine for emergency use on December 2. The country had a coronavirus vaccine task force. The task force planned for health care

HERD IMMUNITY

Vaccines give individual people protection against a disease. When many people in a community get a vaccine, the disease cannot spread easily. This is called herd immunity. Not everyone is able to get a vaccine. Some people have allergic reactions. Pregnant women are unable to get certain vaccines. Herd immunity helps protect these people.

workers and older people to receive the vaccine first. These groups began receiving the approved vaccine on December 8.

RUSSIA

On August 11, Russia announced its scientists had developed a vaccine. It was called Sputnik V. Volunteers in phases one and two showed immunity. They did not have any major side effects.

A health care official in Russia approved Sputnik V for use. Phase three trials had not yet started. Scientists around the world thought this was risky. The vaccine had not been tested on a large group. There could be unknown side effects. Dr. Paul Offit is an American vaccine researcher. He said, "Were I in Russia right now, I would not roll up my sleeves and get this vaccine. . . . It hasn't been adequately tested. I mean, it may be safe and it may work, but why

A volunteer receives Sputnik V during phase three trials.

take that chance? Why do you have

to be lucky?"[5]

Phase three trials for Sputnik V began on

August 25. Forty thousand people in Russia

and Belarus were given the vaccine during

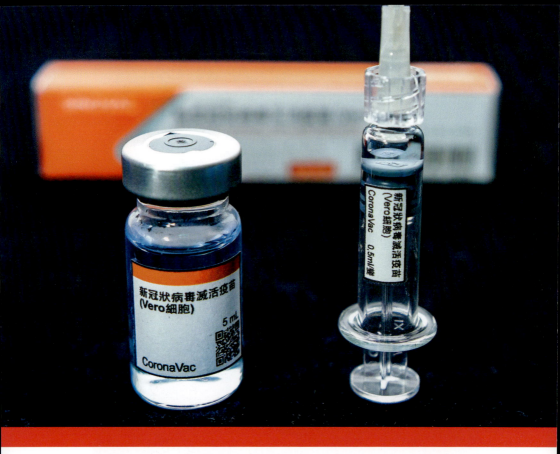

CoronaVac was available for emergency use in China in July 2020.

phase three. Sputnik V continued to be used in Russia.

CHINA

A Chinese company created the vaccine CoronaVac. In July 2020, China approved it for emergency use. It was given to high-risk people such as health care workers.

Other scientists around the world did not think it was safe. Phase three trials had not finished. There was no way tell how well the vaccine worked. Officials continued to give the vaccine to Chinese citizens. They still did not know if CoronaVac was safe and effective.

Countries around the world struggled with a shared problem. They wanted to quickly provide their citizens with a vaccine. But they also needed time to make sure it was safe and effective.

CHAPTER FOUR

HOW WILL THE PANDEMIC END?

Companies continued researching vaccines throughout 2020. By November, six vaccines had been approved for limited use in different countries. Eleven were in phase three trials. Many more were in earlier testing phases.

The pandemic worsened in late 2020. The United States saw a record in new

Hospitals were overwhelmed with COVID-19 patients as new cases continued to rise.

daily cases on December 4. More than 227,000 people were newly diagnosed with COVID-19. Officials looked to vaccines with hope. Yet they also worried about public trust in vaccines.

PUBLIC CONCERNS

Some people did not trust vaccines before the pandemic. They are afraid of side effects. Some people think that vaccines cause autism. But this is not true. Scientists test vaccines to make sure they are safe.

Others might not get vaccines because they are not worried about the disease. They may think the chances of getting sick are low. Or they may believe that even if they get sick, the disease is not serious. Some parents held measles parties during a New York City measles outbreak in 2019. Recovering from measles gives lifetime

Vaccines that are given to the public have been tested to make sure they are safe and effective.

immunity to the disease. But measles can

be deadly. The vaccine is a much safer way

to protect children.

People also worried about how

quickly the COVID-19 vaccine was being

developed. The Pew Research Center did
a survey in September 2020. Seventy-eight
percent of Americans thought the vaccine
was being made too quickly. They
wondered if it would be safe.

Some Americans surveyed said they
would not get a vaccine because they did
not think they needed it. Public opinion
about the dangers of COVID-19 was
shaped in part by President Trump's
response to the pandemic. Public health
officials recommended ways to keep safe
during the pandemic. They told people
to wear masks to slow the spread. They

Many stores in the United States required customers to wear masks to slow the spread of COVID-19.

recommended that people and businesses

practice social distancing. President

Trump did not think the virus was that

severe. He did not always wear a mask

when around other people. He wanted

businesses and schools to reopen. As a result of these mixed messages from different national leaders, US citizens disagreed about how dangerous the virus really was.

POLITICS AND VACCINES

US opinion of a COVID-19 vaccine changed during the pandemic. In May 2020, 72 percent of US adults said they were willing to get a vaccine when it became available. This dropped to 51 percent of adults by September.

One reason for this decline was politics. The 2020 presidential election was in

The pandemic was a major issue during the 2020 presidential election between President Donald Trump (left) and Joe Biden (right).

November. People wanted to know how

Trump and his challenger, Joe Biden, would

handle the pandemic. The promise of a

vaccine became a political issue. Medical

companies rejected pressure to have a

vaccine ready by Election Day. They stated

they would only seek FDA approval after

thoroughly testing a vaccine. They wanted Americans to trust the finished vaccines.

In September, Trump promised a vaccine by the end of 2020. "We'll have manufactured at least 100 million vaccine doses before the end of the year," he said. "Hundreds of millions of doses will be available every month. We expect to have

MULTIPLE VACCINES

Many COVID-19 vaccines were being researched at once. Having more than one working vaccine can be helpful. A vaccine may work better for certain groups. For example, one vaccine may be more effective for older people. Another might work better in younger people.

enough vaccines for every American by April."[6]

But other government officials were not so sure. The director of the CDC, Dr. Robert Redfield, thought it was possible for limited doses to be available in November. He said, "If you're asking me when is it going to be generally available to the American public so we can . . . get back to our regular life, I think we're probably looking at [mid] 2021."[7]

The pandemic was an important issue. Biden won the 2020 presidential election. It would be up to his administration to distribute the vaccine.

ENDING THE PANDEMIC

Finding a vaccine is the first step to ending a pandemic. Then the vaccine needs to be distributed. Many people within a country need to get the vaccine before everybody

COVAX

COVID-19 affected countries around the world. Whichever country developed a vaccine first would likely help its own citizens first. WHO created COVAX, a plan to distribute a vaccine to every country. It wanted to make sure poorer countries would have a vaccine. More than 170 countries had signed COVAX. President Trump did not think that WHO handled the pandemic well. The United States did not sign COVAX during Trump's presidency.

is protected. Operation Warp Speed estimated the first batch of vaccines could cover 3 to 5 percent of the US population. Government officials would decide who would get the vaccine.

The CDC kept close watch on the situation. Officials were hopeful that a vaccine would eventually be available to everyone. They told people to continue practices such as wearing masks and social distancing. With vaccines in progress and people working together to slow the spread, officials were confident the pandemic would come to an end.

antibodies

proteins made by the body to protect against bacteria and viruses

contagious

able to be spread by direct or indirect contact

distributed

given to many people

inject

to give a medication by a needle and syringe

pandemic

an outbreak of disease that occurs over a wide area

proteins

chemicals that are the building blocks of living things

recalled

called to return a product to a company because of safety issues or other reasons

respiratory

related to the process of breathing

SOURCE NOTES

CHAPTER ONE: WHAT IS A VACCINE?

1. Quoted in Katie Kerwin McCrimmon, "Viruses 101: Why the New Coronavirus Is So Contagious and How We Can Fight It," *UCHealth*, March 17, 2020. www.uchealth.org.

2. Quoted in McCrimmon, "Viruses 101."

CHAPTER TWO: HOW DID COVID-19 VACCINE RESEARCH BEGIN?

3. Quoted in "How Soap Suds Kill the Coronavirus," *Health Matters*, 2020. www.healthmatters.nyp.org.

4. Quoted in "Remarks by President Trump on Vaccine Development," *The White House*, May 15, 2020. www.whitehouse.gov.

CHAPTER THREE: WHAT BREAKTHROUGHS DID RESEARCHERS MAKE?

5. Quoted in Patrick Reevell and Sony Salzman, "Russia Announces Expanded Trials for Coronavirus Vaccine Approved 10 Days Ago," *ABC News*, August 20, 2020. www.abcnews.go.com.

CHAPTER FOUR: HOW WILL THE PANDEMIC END?

6. Quoted in "Remarks by President Trump in Press Briefing," *The White House*, September 18, 2020. www.whitehouse.gov.

7. Quoted in Berkeley Lovelace Jr. and Noah Higgins-Dunn, "Trump Says U.S. Will Manufacture Enough Coronavirus Vaccine Doses for Every American by April," *CNBC*, September 18, 2020. www.cnbc.com.

FOR FURTHER RESEARCH

BOOKS

Douglas Hustad, *World Leaders During COVID-19*. Minneapolis, MN: Abdo, 2021.

Anne Rooney, *You Wouldn't Want to Live Without Vaccinations!* New York, NY: Scholastic, 2015.

Shannon Stocker, *Finding the Helpers*. Ann Arbor, MI: Cherry Lake, 2021.

INTERNET SOURCES

"COVID-19 (Coronavirus) Vaccine: Get the Facts," *Mayo Clinic*, October 20, 2020. www.mayoclinic.org.

"How to Protect Yourself & Others," *CDC*, November 4, 2020. www.cdc.gov.

"See Coronavirus Restrictions and Mask Mandates for All 50 States," *New York Times*, December 2, 2020. www.nytimes.com.

WEBSITES

Centers for Disease Control and Prevention
www.cdc.gov

The Centers for Disease Control and Prevention (CDC) updates Americans about health guidelines as well as outbreaks of diseases such as COVID-19.

National Institutes of Health
www.nih.gov/coronavirus

The National Institutes of Health (NIH) is a government agency that conducts medical and public health research, including research on COVID-19.

USA.gov: Coronavirus
www.usa.gov/coronavirus

The USA.gov Coronavirus page provides up-to-date information about the US government's response to the COVID-19 pandemic.

INDEX

IMAGE CREDITS

ABOUT THE AUTHOR

Fran Hodgkins is an award-winning author of many books for young readers. Two of her titles have been selected by the Junior Library Guild, and one received the Eureka! Award from the California Reading Association. Her nonfiction books are about science, animals, and nature. A native of Massachusetts, she lives in Maine.